Song of a Dove

A Christmas Story

Heather Dragoman

WestBow Press books may be ordered through booksellers or by contacting:

WestBow Press
A Division of Thomas Nelson & Zondervan
1663 Liberty Drive
Bloomington, IN 47403
www.westbowpress.com
1 (866) 928-1240

ISBN: 978-1-9736-0834-9 (sc)
ISBN: 978-1-9736-0835-6 (e)

Library of Congress Control Number: 2017916691

Print information available on the last page.

WestBow Press rev. date: 10/15/2018

WestBow
PRESS®
A DIVISION OF THOMAS NELSON
& ZONDERVAN

To my daughter Jessica, who sat on my knee with a purple pastel to, in her words, "help mommy make the pictures." You were only three when you made this one, all by yourself. Your star is on the cover. You are my eternal inspiration. So much love, mom

Song of a Dove

In the still, deep quiet of evening,
The golden sun was already gone.
It was down beneath the hills where sheep lay in slumber,
Not to be back until dawn.

Swift and silent, and gentle in flight,
A dove was on her way home,
But weary of wing thought it best if she rest
In an old olive tree by a road.

"Olive tree," sang the dove, "You are precious and strong. Your shelter is welcome and warm."

The tree whispered, "Welcome, wee feathered one,
For I am feeling alone.

It's quiet," he said, "now that dark is about.
Many travelers have hurried by,
With carts and mules, and children and all.
It's a funny thing, I wonder why."

"Strange too," cooed the bird, "some shining men,
In robes and wise of eye,
Are headed this way in caravan
Along route where I fly."

The two settled themselves to sleep on that night,
With no knowing of what was to come.

Stars brightened and glistened,
There was no sound when they listened.
Night's dark was at hand;
Day was done.

Presently, "clop, clip—clop, clip—clop,"
Echoed small hooves on the road.
A man and a donkey were long left behind,
With a woman astride, traveling slow.

The donkey brayed and nodded his head.
The man touched the lady's knee.
They pulled to a halt and he helped her down
To the ground on unsteady feet.

Washed by a wish from the wondering moon,
Tears glistened in way—weary eyes.
One made its way with a glint to the ground,
Lost to a lingering sigh.

Whispered the dove to the donkey, "Kind sir,
Please tell us why she weeps.
Why do you travel so late in the eve,
And why so unsteady her feet?"

"Need I to gentle my sway," brayed he,
"Sure footed I trod and slow,
No matter the dark, no matter alone,
My master desires it so.

You see, a baby is coming of holy birth.
The woman's time is near.
She needs to rest. The journey is long,
And that's why her eye sheds the tear."

With the woman beside, no longer astride,
Leaning on withers of shaggy brown,
On they went, step, step, and step
Into a sleeping town.

Deep was the sky like an indigo sea.
The moon sailed across on its way,
Twinkling on dewdrops frozen in frost
That were sprinkled in magic array.

A musical sound like wee bells, "Ching, ching,"
Danced with the leaves that night.
The dove gazed up through sleepy eyes,
To a shimmering mystical light.

A single star swept across the sky,
With a tail of streaming gold.
It lit a trail on the frosty ground
Across those hills of old.

Awed by the sight, the dove took flight,
And joined the sheep on the hill.
"Whatever has happened?" chirped the dove,
"And what have you seen? Please tell!"

The slumbering sheep were no longer asleep.
They were restless and in quite a stir.
More than willing, they burst into telling
All they had seen and heard.

"Heaven flew through its doors, right here on this hill,
And beckoned our keepers away!
Divine are the guardians keeping us now,
A mystery we cannot explain.

Celestial hosts in golden hue,
Made the ground in purple glow.
They circled singing with ringing love,
Like wide spread wings of a mother dove!"

"Our keepers took with them a ewe and her lamb,
As gifts for a new Baby King.
She happily went, for such an event
Brings honor to all living things."

"I could sing too," purred the dove, and she went
In the way of the wandering star.
It led her to a hill hollow nook,
With a cozy little barn.

She slipped inside, with the animals there.
"Coo, coo," she said as she came.
"Hush, hush!" said the others in excited reply,
"Or our masters may not let us stay.

Banished are we to this side of the barn.
We heard a baby cry.
A beautiful meeting, between God and man,
Is glowing on the other side."

"I'll fly and see," said the tiny bird. In a whisper she flitted away,
Through the rafters till she saw where the Holy Baby lay.

Then gently, gently in hushaby tones, she cooed endearingly sweet,
Until the Baby closed His eyes and drifted off to sleep.

The latch on the door between stalls was ajar. The handle was below.
She lit upon it. She weighed just enough to make that latch let go.

The door swung wide. The animals spied, in wide—eyed wondering awe.
There in the hay a Baby lay, the sleeping Son of God.

The dove felt the flutter of an angel bright,
"Won't you spread the jubilant news?"

"I will!" she chimed with radiant joy,
And out into the dawn light she flew!

She sang to the tree, her sheltering friend,
And to the sheep who had pointed the way,
And to the travelers both near and far,
The ones still following the magnificent star.

Her pure song still chimes. If you listen with care,
You may hear it in every land;

"Peace is anew in the heart of a Child,

And love is eternal." Amen

Printed in the United States
By Bookmasters